CUENTO
DE LUZ

To my two brothers: the big one, and the middle-sized one.

— Roberto Aliaga —

The Little Golden Key

Text © 2015 Roberto Aliaga
Illustrations © 2015 Dani Padrón
This edition © 2015 Cuento de Luz SL
Calle Claveles, 10 | Urb. Monteclaro | Pozuelo de Alarcón | 28223 | Madrid | Spain
www.cuentodeluz.com
Title in Spanish: La llavecita dorada
English translation by Jon Brokenbrow

ISBN: 978-84-16078-78-3

Printed by Shanghai Chenxi Printing Co., Ltd. July 2015, print number 1526-4

FSC
www.fsc.org
MIX
Paper from
responsible sources
FSC® C007923

THE LITTLE GOLDEN KEY

ROBERTO ALIAGA   DANI PADRÓN

One Saturday morning, after washing behind their ears and having their breakfast, the Mouse brothers set off in search of adventure.

All three of them were happy and smiling: the big one, the middle-sized one, and the little one.

"I want to go and pick apples!"
said the biggest one.
    "I want to pick poppies!"
said the middle-sized one.
    "Well I . . ."
said the littlest one,
    "I want that little piece of the sun
that's fallen onto the ground!"

It was true. There, right next to the path,
something was glittering. But it wasn't
a piece of the sun. What a pity!

It was a key. A little golden key,
just lying there on the ground.

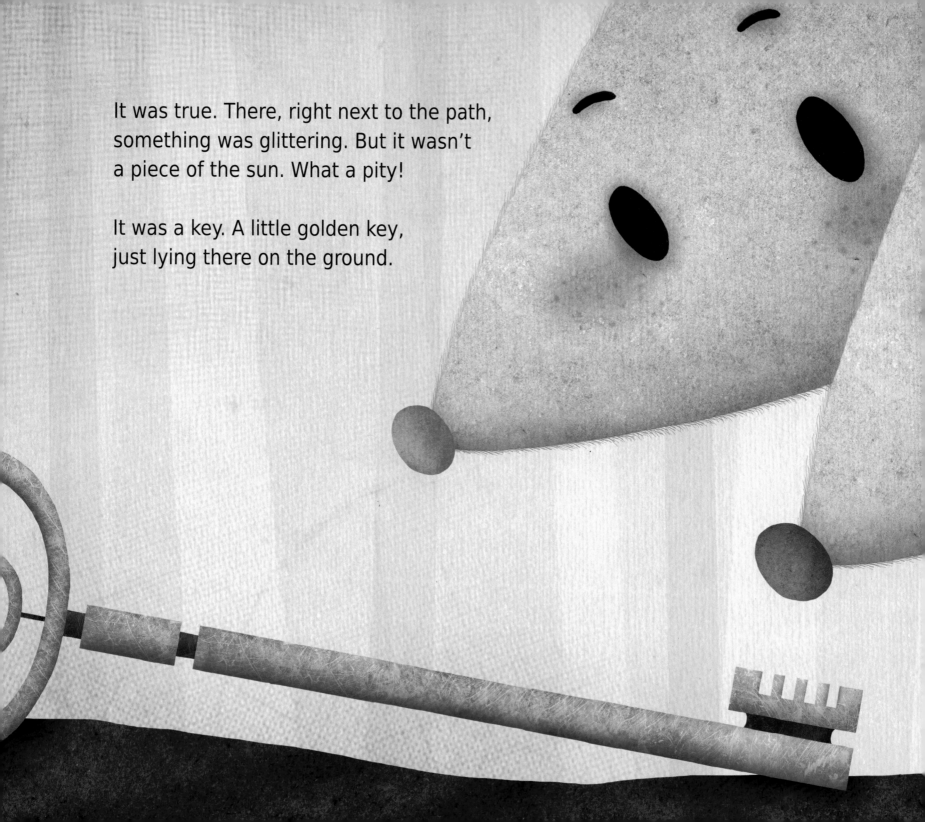

But what did it open?

"I've got it! I've got it!"
Shouted the smallest mouse.
"It looks like it's made of gold,
so I think it must be the key . . .
to a pirate's treasure chest!"

His brothers clapped their paws
at such a brilliant idea,
and all three of them began
to dig holes in the ground.

They found an old, heavy chest,
but however hard they tried,
the golden key wouldn't
open the lock.

"Hang on, I've got it!" shouted the middle-sized mouse.
"It's a very old key; I'm sure it opens the door of an old castle!"

His brothers clapped their paws at such a brilliant idea, and all three of them climbed to the top of the very tallest tree.

Far, far away they saw a castle,
but its lock was so big, it would
have swallowed up the
key in a single gulp.

"I've got it! I've got it!"
shouted the oldest mouse.
"It's got a smiley face! Look!
It must be the key to happiness!"

His brothers clapped their paws at such a brilliant idea. But where could they find happiness, to see if the key would fit?

As none of the mice could find the answer, they decided to run home so that they could ask a grown-up.

Their mom was at the entrance to their nest, looking down at the ground with a sad expression on her face. But when she saw the key, her eyes lit up. "Thank goodness you've found it! Where was it? I must have dropped it without realizing!"

Mom took the little golden key, and used it to open
the door to their nest. A nest full of treasure . . .
that was nearly as big as a castle . . .
and where, as soon as you came in
through the door, you could feel the
happiness in the air.